NAME

DATE

FROM

THOMAS KINKADE

A Child's Christmas

AT

St. Nicholas Circle

Written by Douglas Kaine McKelvey

Thomas Nelson, Inc.
Nashville

Published in Nashville, Tennessee, by Tommy Nelson™,
a division of Thomas Nelson, Inc.

Designed by Koechel Peterson & Associates.

Library of Congress Cataloging-in-Publication Data

McKelvey, Douglas Kaine.
    A child's Christmas at St. Nicholas Circle/featuring the art of
Thomas Kinkade ; written by Douglas Kaine McKelvey.
        p.   cm.
    Summary: When her brother mistakes a lost child for the special
visitor for whom the town is waiting one Christmas Eve, Katie and
her family experience the meaning of the holiday in a special way.
    ISBN 0-8499-5883-0
    [1. Christmas Fiction. 2. Christian life Fiction.] 1. Kinkade,
Thomas 1958- ill. II. Title.
PZ7.M4786744Ch 1999   99-36896
[E]—dc21   CIP

Printed in the United States of America

00 01 02 03 04 LBM 9 8 7 6 5 4 3

List of Paintings

The Thomas Kinkade paintings used in this book are listed below
in the order which they appear, beginning on page 2.

B eside the road that winds through the hills to St. Nicholas Circle, there stands a painted wooden sign engraved with the date, "December 24, 1918." Everyone who was alive on that day in our town still remembers it as clear as yesterday. It was the Christmas of our very Important Guest.

When I was a child, my father was the stationmaster at St. Nicholas Circle. The trains ran there every other day. Passengers on their way to more important places would sometimes step off for a moment to stretch their legs and enjoy a cup of hot coffee. John Shepherd, my father, was famous up and down the Southfork line for his good hospitality, his steaming coffee, and his wife's cookies.

Little Henry, my brother, was six years old, four years younger than I was. We lived in a cozy little cottage on the edge of town. During the Christmas holidays, we often begged Papa to wake us early so we could ride with him through the sleepy lanes to the station. I remember how our horse Junie tossed her mane in the cold December air.

As we neared the edge of town that Christmas Eve morning, the soft lights of the homes and churches sparkled through the icicles that hung from the trees. Here and there people were beginning to stir in the lanes. Papa started singing Christmas carols in a booming voice that would make angels cringe. "Join in Katie," he said with a grin, but I was giggling too hard to sing.

A light snow was falling when we reached the station. Papa sat down at his telegraph and sent out a signal to check the weather up the line.

Henry and I stayed on the train platform and unwrapped biscuits our mother had packed. A couple of deer stepped cautiously from the still woods behind the station. They lifted their heads and watched us for a moment before heading to the stream for a drink.

"Do you think Mama and Papa bought the doll for you and the drum for me?" Henry said, blinking. His mouth was crammed with biscuit.

"I don't know," I answered. "I don't know if they could afford them."

We finished eating our biscuits.

"Katie?" Henry finally said as the sky around us lightened.

"What, Henry?"

"Are we poor?"

I thought for a moment. "Well, we're not rich or poor. We have a house and food to eat. And Papa has a job."

"But I want the drum so much," Henry said, almost crying. "I want the little silver drum with the toy soldier painted on it."

"I know," I said. "You want the drum as much as I want the little Maria doll. She's the most beautiful doll in the world, with her red dress and golden curls. But whatever we get, we'll act happy, because it will be the best Mama and Papa could buy us. Okay?"

"Okay," Henry said softly.

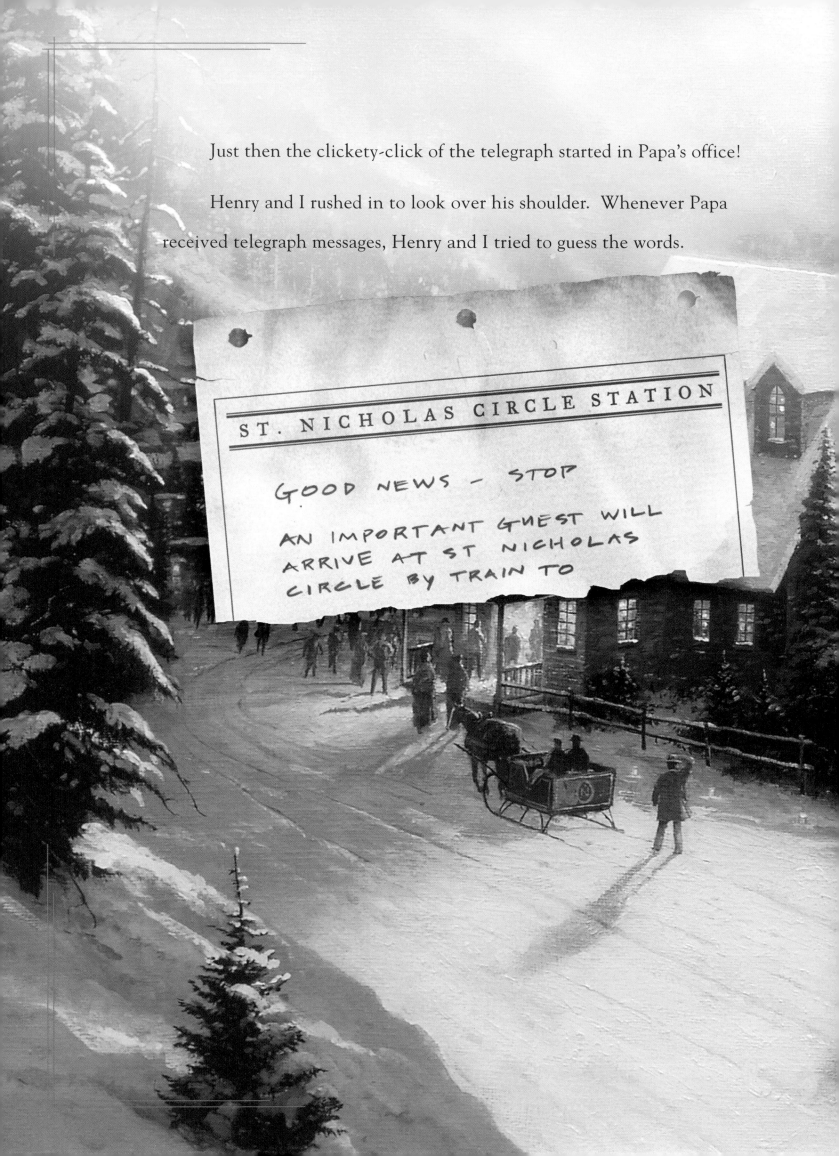

Just then the clickety-click of the telegraph started in Papa's office!

Henry and I rushed in to look over his shoulder. Whenever Papa received telegraph messages, Henry and I tried to guess the words.

ST. NICHOLAS CIRCLE STATION

GOOD NEWS — STOP

AN IMPORTANT GUEST WILL ARRIVE AT ST NICHOLAS CIRCLE BY TRAIN TO

"To-morrow!" Henry whispered.

"To-night!" I whispered back. "The train doesn't run on Christmas."

Henry made a face.

"That's odd," Papa said. "The signal stopped. It must be the weather."

"Who do you think the important guest is?" I whispered to Henry.

"Don't be silly," Henry said. "Santa Claus!"

"On a train?" I asked.

"The ice must have snapped the lines," Papa said. "If so, that's as much message as we'll get today. But I think your guess was right, Katie. Whoever it may be, we can expect an important guest here tonight."

Papa told a few people in town. By the time Henry and I walked home, the streets were buzzing with the news. There were already a dozen different stories about who the Important Guest might be.

"I just hope whoever it is brings lots of toys to the children in St. Nicholas Circle," Henry offered. "Drums for the boys and dolls for the girls."

Mayor Wiggins and his wife Winnie passed us in their carriage. Though they owned the only automobile for miles around, they seldom used it. A horse and carriage were usually fast enough for traveling around our little town. The mayor tipped his hat.

"Spread the word!" he said. "A Christmas Eve reception at our house tonight for the Important Guest! Everyone's invited!"

Papa came home early that afternoon to get cleaned up before the Important Guest arrived. We were late going back to town to meet the train because Henry went out to play without telling anyone. Mama said that one day his disappearing would make her hair gray. We finally found him at the Merritts' house down the road, pulling his bear on a sled. His pants were snow-soaked and filthy.

"I'm pretending I'm marching in a parade," he said. "I just need a drum!"

I saw Mama and Papa trade winks. I knew right then that Henry would get his drum and I would get my doll.

"Go on ahead," Mr. Merritt told us. "We'll get little Henry cleaned up and bring him along with us to the reception."

Mama, Papa, and I arrived just as the train pulled into town. The mayor's treasured car was parked outside, but he, along with half the town, was already crowded into the station. Those left outside mingled near the doors, stamping their feet to keep warm. A few ribbons and homemade "Welcome!" signs were visible. The music teacher, Miss Belle, hurried to pass out song sheets.

I squeezed my way into Papa's office and looked out the window just in time to see a suited gentleman step onto the platform. He had a curious air. He smiled at the people standing nearby, yawned, and slowly bent down to touch his toes.

Before he had fully straightened up, Mayor Wiggins grabbed his hand and shook it joyfully.

"Honored guest!" the mayor said, as wild cheers, blinding flashes, and confetti streamers filled the air behind him. "Let me be the first to welcome you! We've so been looking forward to your visit!"

"Speech! Speech!" everyone shouted to the Important Guest.

"I...I don't know what to say," the man stammered.

"Just say you'll allow us the pleasure of your company at a reception in your honor!" Mayor Wiggins said with a merry smile.

"But...the train...my bags," the Important Guest said.

Just then Miss Belle gave a signal. Half of us launched into "For He's a Jolly Good Fellow." Unfortunately, the song sheets had been mixed up. The other half of the crowd was trying to sing "Joy to the World." It sounded like a two-engine train wreck.

"Who needs talent when you've got enthusiasm, eh?!" the mayor joked, whisking the Important Guest out to his car for a one-block ride to the reception.

I looked for Henry during the crowded reception at the mayor's house afterwards. But I never did find him. People were coming and going in all the rooms, eating and drinking and chattering about the Important Guest.

"He's very mysterious," said one woman hovering near a tray of gingerbread. "I'd skip Christmas to know what's in his suitcases!"

"I helped load his bags into the mayor's car," said a young man standing nearby. "One suitcase popped open. It looked like it was full of a bunch of cleaning brushes."

"Is that so?" the woman answered. "How utterly mysterious!"

I grabbed a piece of gingerbread and went out by the mayor's pond.

Kids were sledding nearby, and a few young couples, too in love to care

about the Important Guest, were ice skating in the moonlight.

"Has anyone seen Henry?" I asked.

"He took his sled and went home already," someone said.

Sure enough, Henry was waiting at the door when the rest of us got home. "Shhhhhh," he said excitedly. "The Important Guest decided to come to our house, and he fell asleep in my bed!"

Mama and Papa and I looked at one another.

"The Important Guest is staying at Mayor Wiggins," I said.

"Nope, he's here!" Henry said, racing down the hall ahead of us. "He was standing in the street, and he was so cold. I gave him my coat and pulled him here on my sled. He ate a lot! Then I let him sleep on my bed. He doesn't talk, though."

We stepped quietly into Henry's room. There, just as Henry had said, a boy of six or seven lay fast asleep. His shirt looked old and dirty, and one of his shoes was too big. But his breathing was light and peaceful.

"Who is he, Henry?" Papa asked, kneeling beside the bed. "Tell me again."

Henry sighed. "He's the Important Guest, Papa!"

"We need to find his parents," Papa said.

Henry furrowed his brow. "He's the Important Guest, and he's staying for Christmas!"

"He must have come off the train during all the commotion," Mama said, stroking the boy's forehead. "Poor dear. Couldn't even talk. Just followed all the people into town."

Papa and I got back into the sleigh and set out for the nearest telephone. It was in the parson's office at Ridge Church, a half mile away. The night felt still and hushed and very important.

When we got there, Papa called the next railroad station down the line while I sat among the sanctuary's flickering candles.

"Merry Christmas, Katie Shepherd," Parson Chambers whispered, sitting down beside me.

"You know," he said after a while, "that little stranger at your house isn't the only important guest ever to make an unexpected appearance in a small town around Christmas."

"But the real Important Guest is at Mayor Wiggins' house," I said. "The little boy at our house can't even talk. We don't know who he is."

"You don't?" the parson said with feigned surprise. "Well, that's very interesting, because I've never seen him, but I think I know a little something about who he is."

"You see, that first and most important Christmas Eve guest once told us: 'Whoever welcomes a little child in my name, welcomes me.' And another time he said 'As you have done unto the least of these, so you have done unto me.'"

"So the boy who can't talk is Jesus?" I asked.

"Not exactly," the parson replied. "How can I explain? If you were standing in line at the candy counter after school and you needed a drink very badly, what would you do?"

"I would ask one of my friends to hold my place in line," I said, "until I came back."

"Very good," the parson said. "You see, that boy and others poor and helpless like him...well, those seem to be the people that Jesus has chosen to hold his place in line."

We sat quietly in the candlelight until Papa returned.

Mama had been right. Papa finally got through to the next station and spoke to the boy's sobbing mother. We learned his name was Matty. He had slipped off the train unnoticed while his mother tended his little sisters, Adeline and Opal. They were traveling to the city in hope of finding work.

We emptied our Christmas stockings the next morning. Matty watched from the corner in quiet wonder as apples, walnuts, and peppermint sticks spilled out. There was a stocking for Matty too, but Henry had to help him with it. When it was time to open our special gifts, I couldn't get the paper off fast enough.

"Henry, look!" I squealed with delight. "It's my doll! It's Maria!"

But Henry was troubled. His lower lip stuck out and the package he held was unopened.

"I want it to be for Matty," he finally said.

Henry carried the package to the corner where Matty sat. "Here, Matty," he said. "This is the way you pull the paper off.…Here's how you hold the sticks." A small sob caught in his voice as he gently encouraged Matty. "See, here's how you play it. There you go." But when they turned to show off the drum a moment later, both of them were beaming.

A minute later there was a knock at the door. I opened it to find a scared little girl and a woman with a whimpering baby. Their clothes were patched and frayed, and they looked so thin and cold I wanted to cry just looking at them. The little girl peeked around her mother at the doll in my arms.

"Merry Christmas. Don't mean to bother you, Miss," the woman said in a voice that sounded very sad and far away. "But is this where my Matty is?" I could see her lip quivering.

I looked down at the new, precious doll in my arms, and I tried to push every other thought away, but it was no use. The harder I tried, the more I could see only a picture of Matty, Adeline, Opal, and their mother, holding Jesus' place in a long, long line. The words of Jesus which the parson had quoted echoed in my head and landed in my heart.

"As you have done unto the least of these, so you have done unto me."

The next thing I knew, my hands were trembling and reaching out like they were someone else's. I watched them place my priceless doll into the little girl's hands. The rest was easy.

"Merry Christmas, Adeline," I said, bending and kissing her on the cheek. "Take good care of Maria! She's very special, just like you!"

Then I turned to the startled woman. "Please come in. My name is Katie Shepherd," I said. "Merry Christmas! You are very important guests. We've been looking forward to your visit!"

Many years later, our Papa passed away. While going through his personal things, Henry and I discovered a rolled up telegraph message in two halves. One half held a yellowed message as familiar as our own names.

The second piece had come several days later after the telegraph line was repaired. It fit together neatly at the tear.

ST. NICHOLAS CIRCLE STATION

GOOD NEWS — STOP

AN IMPORTANT GUEST WILL ARRIVE AT ST NICHOLAS CIRCLE BY TRAIN TO

DAZZLE YOUNG AND OLD ALIKE WITH HIS FEATS OF JUGGLING AND MAGIC — STOP

DON'T MISS THIS ONCE IN A LIFETIME CHANCE TO SEE THE AMAZING MR FAUSTUSS PERFORM JANUARY 17TH — STOP

Our mysterious message had been nothing more than an advertisement for a traveling magician. A magician who never showed up!

Henry and I never told the contents of the message. All that really mattered was that our town had so wonderfully welcomed a mysterious stranger that Christmas Eve. It made no difference who he was. Although, looking back, the brushes in the suitcase gave us a little hint.

If we had learned that Matty and his sisters were important in the eyes of God, then it only made sense to believe that the other unknown guest, whether he was the Prince of England or a traveling brush salesman, was truly important too.

Deep down, it meant that all of us were important.

Now when I recall the story of our Important Guest, I can't help but smile. Isn't it nice to think that, at least once in the history of this world, an unknown stranger might have stumbled into an unexpected place and received the kind of welcome he always deserved?

Even if it was by mistake?

As for Matty, his mother wrote us a letter every year after they settled in the city. She said they had a hard time of it at first, but she found work here and there cleaning houses, and she eventually took a position with a wealthy elderly couple who needed looking after. The couple doted on Matty, Adeline, and Opal like they were their own grandchildren. After a month or two they moved Matty's whole family into their guest quarters.

Once Matty and Adeline and Opal and their mother managed to visit us again at Christmastime. Matty stood at our front window for hours, patiently waiting. It seemed like he knew he was holding Jesus' place in line, and expected him back soon. I thought about that a lot when we got a letter the next May saying Matty had died from a sudden fever.

In the fall of the year, Mama and Papa and Henry and I took the train to visit Adeline and Opal and their mother. We saw them almost every year after that.

I guess I should mention that Henry and Adeline got married and are expecting their third child this June. They live just out of town in a house that Henry built seven years ago, right after they married and he became stationmaster for St. Nicholas Circle. If Henry and Adeline have a girl, Matty and Maria Shepherd will have a new little sister. Adeline tells me her name will be "Katie."

THE END